The Inner City
Mother Goose

Eve Merriam

The Inner City Mother Goose

Illustrated by
David Diaz

Introduction by
Nikki Giovanni

Simon & Schuster Books for Young Readers

SIMON & SCHUSTER BOOKS FOR YOUNG READERS
An imprint of Simon & Schuster Children's Publishing Division
1230 Avenue of the Americas, New York, New York 10020
SIMON & SCHUSTER BOOKS FOR YOUNG READERS
is a trademark of Simon & Schuster.
Book design by Paul Zakris
The text for this book is set in 18-point Journal Text
The illustrations are rendered in acrylic
Manufactured in the United States of America
10 9 8 7 6 5 4 3 2 1

Library of Congress Cataloging-in-Publication Data
Merriam, Eve.
The inner city Mother Goose / by Eve Merriam ; illustrated by
David Diaz ; introduction by Nikki Giovanni. — 3rd edition.
p.   cm.
Summary: Poems inspired by traditional nursery rhymes depict
the grim reality of inner city life, including such topics as crime,
drug abuse, unemployment, and inadequate housing.
ISBN 0-689-80677-9
1. City and town life—United States—Juvenile poetry.   2. Mother
Goose—Parodies, imitations, etc.   3. Children's poetry, American.
[1. City and town life—Poetry.   2. American poetry.]   I. Diaz,
David, ill.   II. Title.
PS3525.E639I5   1996   811'.54—dc20   95-22553   CIP   AC

Remembering
Jesse B. Semple's daddy
—E. M.

For Troy Viss,
"Kings of the Playground"
—D. D.

CONTENTS

The Inner
City Me

"**O**nce upon a time . . ." I like that. It indicated that day was ending, evening supper had been eaten, utensils put away, most likely that the adults were getting ready to light a pipe or a cigarette and sit back to watch the sun spread her final red glow over the earth. "Once upon a time . . ." The children could gather near us as they were included in these tales. The storyteller told of great deeds or some foolishness. . . . A lesson was to be learned. Maybe the children even prompted a story, asking for their favorite trickster or hero. The fire glowed, the sliver of a new moon shown down. . . . All was right with the world.

But when people had a bit of news to pass, a bit of gossip to share, a warning to give, things had to go quicker. A way to pass the word had to be coded in case there was someone who would take the message back to the king or the landowner or the overseer or the master. A message had to be sent that sounded innocent enough but to the involved would give the proper warning. What we now refer to as children's stories started out as warnings, as laughter at the powerful, as a way of passing the truth along.

Who, indeed, is Little Boy Blue? He must have meant something when the women passed the word at market; when the men, watching the sheep, mentioned him. "Under the haystack fast asleep." Was he the owner who didn't have to sit in the cold and the dark? It's hard to imagine he was a worker. Workers never celebrated those who did not do their fair share. Eve Merriam took the spirit of Mother Goose to the inner city to give voice to those who were being silenced. She did not have the luxury of code. She had the moral indignation of a just cause. . . . Agony should not be ignored. Mother Goose emerged among the peasants to let them know they were not incorrect in their perceptions; Merriam gave voice to the inner city to let them know there are some who hear.

Had the powers that be understood that the peasants were laughing at them, were laughing at the airs they put on, their manners, their affectations, the prissy ways the gentry goes about its business, heads would, indeed, have rolled. But the powers that be never listen carefully, so a rhyme was passed down, and it is still good.

People objected to Merriam's inner city. Not because it existed, but because she protested it. Good for Eve. Good for all of us. There are, indeed, times when there is nothing we can do about the conditions we see, the pain we empathize with, the hopelessness of the situation. But we can acknowledge that it exists. We can say to those inhabiting the neglect of the greedy, "You do exist and I think it's wrong." Good for words that allow us to reach across the ages and find a way to connect the possibilities of human beings.

The children have that old expression, "Sticks and stones can break my bones, but words will never hurt me. . . ." but I know, and you know, that that's not true. Sticks and stones are easily forgotten; it is the words that stay with us. The hurtful words that make us less than human; the words used to describe Black Americans; the words used to justify the inhumane treatment of Native Americans. Words will always be stronger than swords because swords can only harm our bodies. Words can harm our souls.

It is good to reread the words of Eve Merriam, to relive the struggle, to allow words to carry some healing. *The Inner City Mother Goose* carries a truth that touches the inner city me. We are all a part of this civilization. We need some truth to make this passage from birth to death a more gentle situation.

NIKKI GIOVANNI
Blacksburg, Virginia
May 1996

Introduction to the 1982 Edition

Hushabye Baby on the Tree Top,
When the Wind blows
The Cradle will rock;
When the Bough breaks
The Cradle will fall,
Down tumbles Baby,
Cradle and all.

Mother Goose rhymes have long been part of our folk tradition; they are centuries old and nobody knows for certain who wrote them originally. As our most familiar lullabies and chants, we take their often surreal images for granted without examining what the words are saying. "Mistress Mary, quite contrary, how does your garden grow? With silver bells and cockle shells, and pretty maids all in a row." "One, Two, buckle my shoe; Three, Four, shut the door . . ." "Sing a song of sixpence, a pocket full of rye, four-and-twenty blackbirds baked in a pie; when the pie was opened, the birds began to sing; was not that a dainty dish, to set before the King?"

The cast of characters is vivid: Simple Simon who met a pie man going to the fair; the Old Woman who lived in a shoe; rub-a-dub-dub, Three Men in a tub; Tom, Tom, the piper's son; "Hey Diddle Diddle, the Cat and the Fiddle, the Cow jumped over the moon, the Little Dog laughed to see such sport, and the Dish ran away with the Spoon." The rhythms are emphatic and solid, just right for bouncing baby on a knee or for playing a clap-hands game. Mother Goose in the nursery.

But there is another side to the old rhymes. When they first became known, in the seventeenth and eighteenth centuries, they were not considered nonsensical verses for little children. They were taken as social and political commentary on the vice-ridden times. Little Jack Horner, for instance, who "put in his thumb and pulled out a plum and said 'What a good boy am I'" was rumored to be a clever real estate operator who had his finger in some juicy payola pies. In the case of "Who Killed Cock Robin?" ("'I' said the sparrow, 'With my bow and arrow'") the gossip in government circles during the rule of Oliver Cromwell was that Robin was Sir Robert Walpole, secretary of the treasury. Other real life personnel were said to be involved in "There was a crooked man and he walked a crooked mile, he found a crooked sixpence against a crooked stile; he bought a crooked cat, which caught a crooked mouse, and they all lived together in a little crooked house." Supposedly the crooked man was General Sir Alexander Leslie of Scotland, the crooked sixpence was England's King Charles I, and the crooked stile was the disputed border between their two countries.

So when I wanted to comment about some social and political issues in our time, I was following an old tradition in using Mother Goose characters. What modern situations would they face, and where would they live?

Daily our world becomes more and more urbanized and overcrowded, and inner cities are the heart of our urban structure. Suffering from benign and not so benign neglect, they are also resilient with the strength and humor of people who live there. If our inner cities survive, we will all survive. If allowed to deteriorate further, they may, like Humpty Dumpty, have such a great fall that all the King's horses and all the King's men (or all the presidents and congressmen) may not be able to put it together again.

When I first wrote *The Inner City Mother Goose* in 1969 I took up a number of distressingly familiar topics that I felt we dare not close our eyes to: inadequate housing, unemployment, rats, cockroaches, crime and violence in the streets, noise pollution, graft—including police corruption, insufficient public transportation, cutbacks in funding for essential community services. In the intervening years such problems have not disappeared, they have only intensified. It seems to me it would not only be morally wrong, it would be politically tragic to gloss over these areas and refuse to recognize their reality, for if we do we will not be able to redeem our cities and thereby our civilization.

Placing Mother Goose inside the inner city, Mistress Mary became "Mary, Mary, Urban Mary, how does your sidewalk grow?" Hushabye Baby on the Tree Top moved to the top floor where the project elevator doesn't work anymore. The satiric verses I wrote would not eliminate any of the dismaying conditions, but I hoped would make people more aware. Recalling how my next-door neighbor had her pocketbook wrenched from her at knifepoint in broad daylight, I changed "Jack be nimble, Jack be quick, Jack jump over the candlestick" to "Jack be nimble, Jack be quick, Snap the blade and give it a flick." While it wouldn't necessarily forestall future muggings, it might make pedestrians a bit more alert when walking.

What I didn't expect was that such verses would cause the book to be banned, and that over a period of years, it would become just about the most banned book in the country.

Why? Is it because of the down-to-earth language?

There is one epithet in the book. I had used almost the whole of an original Mother Goose rhyme.

Boys and girls come out to play,
The moon doth shine as bright as day.
Leave your supper and leave your sleep,
And join your playfellows in the street.
Come with a whoop and come with a call:

Instead of continuing with the old verse, I broke it off and added a line that contained an extremely vulgar, if commonly used, thirteen-letter word. Could that alone account for the book's widespread banning?

It may be more germane that one critical reader wrote in after hearing me read some of the verses on a national news broadcast, "I never believed in stirring things up as this book may do." Throughout the decade of the seventies, censorship mounted. A teacher at a California high school who lent the book to a student who asked to borrow it was fired; the student's mother was so infuriated by the contents that she burned the book. In some social studies resource centers, where the book had been available, it was put under lock and key. In some high school libraries, students had to sign a special slip to be allowed to read it. Even colleges came under attack: as a result of learning that the book was used in the curriculum at Penn State's Capitol campus, a state senator introduced a resolution to investigate the education curriculum at all state universities. The Knights of Columbus condemned it, stating that "this book is obscene and degrading in that it glorifies the decadence in our society, emphasizing prejudice and bigotry. Continued exposure of this type of material to students of elementary education will cause them to become cynical and frustrate the workings of a Christian community." The mayor of Minneapolis inveighed against the book. In Baltimore, the city comptroller declared at a public meeting that the book was "part of a nationwide plot to just cause this nation to disintegrate." In Buffalo, a grand jury investigation was called, and the investigation halted only when the book was removed from all Model City school libraries. The Patrolmen's Benevolent Association of Boston denounced the book as "anti-police, anti-law-and-order, and anti-government" demanding that every copy be removed from the entire public library systems of Boston and eastern Massachusetts. A congressman put his remarks into the Congressional Record: "This book has an evil theme. 'Jack be nimble, Jack be quick, Snap the blade and give it a flick.' This represents an outright invitation to a youth reading this line to get a knife if he does not already have one, and nimbly and quickly ready it for use."

It would be wondrously simple if the banning of my book could remove crime and temptation; I would certainly consider sacrificing it on the altar of such high ideals. I think rather that the situation is otherwise, and that the television official in Baltimore who broadcast three editorials supporting the book may possibly be more on target in declaring that "it deals with the truth. Perhaps this is why it offends some of us."

The Inner City Mother Goose was published by Simon & Schuster and sold nearly 100,000 copies. The book served as the basis for the 1971–72 Broadway musical Inner City. Since then I have revised and updated the text considerably and it is now the foundation for the new musical Street Dreams. This special edition contains many verses never before published. However, I have not censored myself by removing the single epithet or any of the themes that originally came under attack.

EVE MERRIAM
New York
August 1982

Jeremiah Obadiah

I'm Jeremiah Obadiah, puff, puff, puff,
When I take the messages I snuff, snuff,
    snuff.
Everywhere you look around, it's tough,
    tough, tough,
Everybody's hustling and it's rough, rough,
    rough.

When I go to school by day I snore, snore,
    snore,
What's the use of lesson books to score,
    score, score?
Teacher passes by me and she sniff, sniff,
    sniff,
Come on, teach, you want to try a whiff,
    whiff, whiff?

Got to get a pass so class can be dismiss,
Got to get a pass to go and piss, piss, piss.
I'm Jeremiah Obadiah, where do I get my
    stuff?
Right out in the schoolyard puff, puff, puff.

The Nub of the Nation

This is the nub of the nation:
In that nation is a city,
In that city is a ghetto.
In that ghetto is a street,
On that street there is a house,
In that house there is a stair,
On that stair there is a door,
Through that door there waits a room,
In that room there is a chair,
On that chair there is a person
Sitting staring there.

Sitting staring there
On the broken chair,
Chair in the cockroach room,
Room on the worn-out stair,
Stair in the no-care house,
House on the drop-dead street,
Street in the ghetto rot,
Ghetto rooted in the city,
City spreading everywhere:
And this is the nub of the nation.

Simple Simon

Simple Simon
Met a high man
In the government.

Said Simple Simon
To the high man,
"How are taxes spent?"

"Billions," said the high man
"For an antimissile system
That's bound
To be obsolete
Before it ever
Gets off the ground."

"But that's ridiculous!"
Said Simple Simon.
"If people knew,
They'd make a fuss."

"True," said the high man,
"And when you take into account
That for just about half that amount
Everybody could have a decent job
And a house in a decent neighborhood."

"Fantastic," said Simple Simon.
"I don't believe it."

Said the high man,
"Good."

Mary, Mary

Mary, Mary,
Urban Mary,
How does your sidewalk grow?
With chewing gum wads
And cigarette butts
And popsicle sticks
And potato chip bags
And candy wrappers
And beer cans
And broken bottles
And crusts of pizza
And coffee grounds
And burnt-out light bulbs
And a garbage
    strike all in a row.

Diddle Diddle Dumpling

Diddle diddle dumpling, my son Juan
Went to bed with his trousers on
And with the rest of the family
Sharing a single-room occupancy.

Star Light, Star Bright

Star light,
Star bright,
Is it true the stars
Are clear at night?
Do they shine
Like traffic lights in lines,
Or do they glow
Like neon signs?
Do they hurt your eyes
Like the flashlight's glare
When you're told to halt
With your hands in the air?
Are they white as the clinic's
Overhead light?
Do they burn out at dawn?
Turn on every night?

Now I Lay Me Down to Sleep

Now I lay me down to sleep
I pray the double lock will keep;
May no brick through the window break,
And no one rob me till I wake.

There Is a Lady

There is a lady
Who lives on the street
With bags for her body
And bags for her feet.

In winter she puts on
Bags and more bags,
In summer she adds on
Layers of rags.

Some days she's laughing,
Some days she cries,
Who knows if she's crazy,
Who knows if she's wise.

Hark, Hark

HARK, HARK
   The dogs do BARK
The neighbors YELL
   The buses GRIND
The babies CRY
   The telephones RING
The jet planes FLY
   The bongos BONG
The car horns HONK
   The taxis SCREECH
The radio's ON
   The TV's HIGH
The subway ROARS
   Rock-and-roll POURS from the
     record stores
The old women MUTTER along the gutter
the rats SQUEAK
   The flies BUZZ
   only the roaches quietly crawl

Lucy Locket

Lucy Locket lost her pocket,
Kitty Fisher found it;
Not a penny was there in it,
Only ribbon round it.
   Kitty got mad and cut Lucy up.

Jack Be Nimble
Jack Be Quick

Jack be nimble
Jack be quick
Snap the blade
And give it a flick.

Grab the purse
It's easily done
Then just for kicks
Just for fun
Plunge the knife
And cut
And run . . .

Take-a-Tour, Take-a-Tour, Congressman

Take-a-tour,
Take-a-tour,
Congressman,

Cover the ghetto
As fast as
You can:

Whisk through,
Tsk tsk through,
And file under P:

Now you're
An expert
On Poverty.

Boys and Girls Come Out to Play

Boys and girls come out to play,
The moon doth shine as bright as day.
Leave you supper and leave your sleep,
And join your playfellows in the street.
Come with a whoop and come with a call:
Up, motherfuckers, against the wall.

What Are Summer Nights Made Of?

What are summer nights made of, made of?
What are summer nights made of?

Too much heat,
Junk on the street,
Fire alarms,
Patrol cars,
Pickups and payoffs in bars.

What Are Winter Nights Made Of?

What are winter nights made of, made of?
What are winter nights made of?

Not enough heat,
Junk on the street,
Fire alarms,
Patrol cars,
Payoffs and pickups in bars.

Everyone Knows

Everyone knows who I am:
I am the Prince of Fame;
For everywhere the subway goes,
Graffiti mars my name.

You'll Find Mice

You'll find mice, see how they run!
They all ran out from behind the stove
One climbed on the table and down he dove,
Then over the bread box he poked his head
And back to his favorite spot once more
To the bureau drawer that's set out on
　　the floor
For baby's bed.

Ding, Dong, Bell

Ding, dong, bell,
The rat control is on the way,
The sweeper trucks are starting to spray,
The garbage trucks are beginning to hum,
The exterminator may even come!

They've got to disinfect it some,
For the mayor's coming to look today
At daily life in a slum.

Hushabye Baby

Hushabye, baby,
On the top floor,
Project elevator
Won't work anymore.

It comes up to ten
And then starts to stall;
We'll have to walk down, baby,
Carriage and all.

Rub-a-Dub-Dub

Rub-a-dub-dub,
Ceiling's in the tub;
And how do you think it got there?

Water in the tub
On the floor above;
And that's how our ceiling got there.

Here We Go Round

Here we go round the official list,
Official list,
Official list,
Here we go round the official list,
Official list again.

Welfare allowance for shoes this year,
Shoes this year,
Sign right here,
You're entitled to buy brand-new
Half a shoe this year.

Here Am I,
Little Jumping Joan

Here am I,
Little Jumping Joan;
When nobody's with me
I'm all alone.

My daddy's gone,
And my mommy's gone till dark
Strolling with a carriage
In the park.

Lady's baby out
With my mommy all day
While I stay in
By myself and play.

The Recruiting Sergeant

Come here to me, my merry merry men,
Said a sergeant loud and clear;

And the young men all were very
        merry men
And they all came running near
And the flag flew in the air,
And the drummer drummed his share,
And the sergeant spoke of Liberty
And pay and opportunity,
And the boys cried out

Hell no!
We won't go!

The Generals

The Generals in the Pentagon
Are counting up their warheads:
They stockpile to infinity
And then they call for more heads.

Taxi Man

Taxi man, taxi man,
Quick drive me home!
My house is on fire
And my children all—!

Sorry, lady,
Even in an emergency
Cabs don't go to Harlem.

Robin and Richard

Robin and Richard
Two young city men,
Lay in bed
Till the clock struck ten.
Then up started Robin
And looks at the sky,
Oh, brother Richard
The sun's very high.

"No matter," says Richard,
"What time it may be,
There are no jobs now
For you or for me."

"Then, brother Richard,
Let's go out and play.
We'll enjoy
A fine holiday."

"No, brother Robin,
There is no way.
No, brother Robin,
We can't go and play
With no jobs to work on,
No time can be free.
There are no days off
For you and for me."

If Wishes Were Horses, Beggars Would Ride

If wishes were horses, beggars would ride
And rich and poor in peace would abide
If only the poor would smell sweet and
    be neat
And clean up the street
And talk nice and polite
And not publicly fight
And have college degrees
And station wagon keys
And interesting jobs that were also secure
—Or else kept out of sight and learned
    to endure—
There'd be nothing wrong with their just
    being poor.

Sing a Song of Subways

Sing a song of subways,
Never see the sun;
Four-and-twenty people
In a room for one.

When the doors are opened—
Everybody run.

I Had a Little

I had a little TV,
Kept it over there,
Over by the window;
Now the place is bare.

The installment collector
Came to visit me,
And all for the sake of
My little TV.

My Mother Said

My mother said I never would
Turn out to be anything good.
Everything I did she'd say,
"Bad bad girl to disobey.
You'll get in trouble, wait and see,
Don't you come running home to me."
And Father said that if I did,
He'd knock my head with the teapot lid.
School was dumb and the teacher mean,
Along came a man in a limousine.
I jumped inside, was off in a crack,
Tell my mother I'll never come back,
Tell everybody I'll never come back.

Now my belly's tight as a drum
Waiting for the baby to come.
Too late to do anything:
I bought myself a dime-store ring.
I won't give my baby away,
With my baby alone I'll stay
And never ever will I say
You are bad to disobey.
Baby, don't you be mad at me,
We'll have good times, wait and see,
I'll be your mama, I'll be your dad,
We'll laugh and smile and we won't be sad,
And baby, my baby, it won't turn out bad.

Who Killed Nobody?

Who killed nobody?
I, said the policeman,
With my off-duty gun,
I killed no one.

Who saw him die?
I, said his mother,
ai, my son, aii!

Who caught his blood?
I, said another,
For he was a Brother.

Who'll carry the coffin?
We, said his neighbors,
We'll carry the coffin;
We've done it often.

All the people there
Fell a-sighing and a-sobbing
When they heard the bell toll. . . .

They're a highly emotional people,
Tend to fly off the handle,
Said the policeman,
Stroking his off-duty gun
That killed no one.

On TV

On TV
   see the looters run
With whiskey
      and cartons
         of cigarettes,
With wigs
   and sofas
     and TV sets—
  Running
    after
      the merchandise
  All the
    commercials
     advertise
       on TV
         on TV
           on TV
            on TV
             on TV . . .

This Is the Plant
That Was Built

This is the nuclear plant that was built.
There are safety factors built in
to the nuclear plant that was built.
There are locks on the door
And a containment floor
And pipes that are strong
And the air flows along
And a pump to fall back on just in case
And the computer checks everything in
    its place

And that's a good thing because
The leakproof pipes are prone to leak
And the doorlocks don't always totally lock
And the air-cooling system tends to blow
And the sump pump doesn't pump out
    the flow
And the containment floor doesn't contain

So bless the nuclear plant that's built
With a giant computer brain built in
With only the least little space
For a nobody's perfect mistake.

Cherry Stones

Tinker,
Tailor,
Soldier,
Sailor,
Rich man,
Culturally disadvantaged underachiever.

Jack Sprat

Jack Sprat
Is not so fat,
His wife's grown
Very lean:

They used to have food stamps.

Taffy

Taffy is a storeman,
Taffy is a thief;
Taffy overcharges
For a tough piece of beef.

Taffy's cheese is moldy,
His eggs are sold with cracks;
There are seldom more than five
In his six-bottle packs.

His sacks of potatoes
Are sprouting with eyes;
There's hardly any fruit,
But many fruit flies.

His frozen food case
Has a constant leak;
His floor is never swept,
His milk is from last week.

Taffy's stock is low
Yet somehow Taffy thrives;
Taffy offers credit
Till the monthly check arrives.

If

If all the seas were one sea,
What a *great* sea that would be!
If all the slums were one slum,
What a *great* slum that would be!
And if all the axes were one ax,
What a *great* ax that would be!
And if all the men were one man,
What a *great* man that would be!
And if the *great* man took the *great* ax,
And cut down the *great* slum,
And let it fall into the *great* sea—
What a *great* IF that would be!

To Market

To market
Supermarket,
To buy a full quart;

Home again,
Open it:
Measure is short.

Run, Run

Run, run Father, go away:
Welfare worker is due today.

One Misty Moisty Morning

One misty moisty morning
Virus was the weather;
Waiting for the bus to come,
Closed in together.

One began to cough and shake,
Another cursed his mother,
Someone felt up someone,
A day like any other.

One, Two

One, two,
Welfare for you;

Three, four,
Agency door;

Five, six,
Caseworker picks;

Seven, eight,
Investigate;

Nine, ten,
Fill out more forms
and wait in line all over again.

One, two,
Welfare for you;

Three, four,
Agency door;
Five, six,
Caseworker picks;

Seven, eight,
Investigate;

Nine, ten,
Fill out more forms
and wait in line all over again.

Christmas Is Coming

Christmas is coming,
The advertising's fat,
Please to put a dollar
In the old man's hat.
If you haven't got a dollar,
Then half will have to do;
If you haven't got a half a buck,
Then God mug you!

Twelve Rooftops Leaping

12 rooftops leaping
11 windows smashing
10 pipes a-bursting
 9 sirens screaming
 8 phone booths broken
 7 bulbs a-dimming
 6 junkies trading
 5 stolen rings
 4 padlocked stores
 3 slashed tires
 2 cherry bombs

And a scout group planting a tree.

Fee, Fi, Fo, Fum

Fee, fi, fo, fum,
I smell the blood of violence to come;
I smell the smoke that hangs in the air
Of buildings burning everywhere;
Even the rats abandon the city:
The situation is being studied
By a crisis committee.

There Is an Old Woman

There is an old woman who lives by herself
With advertised pet food high on her shelf:
"Meat-flavored, yum yum, for your kitten
    or pup,"
She opens a can and then eats it up.

There Was a Man
and He Had Naught

There was a man and he had naught
And robbers came to rob him,
He shook and shook his empty cup
And thought that it would stop them.

Please go away,
This crime won't pay,
It isn't worth a fight.

They tore his clothes
And punched his nose
And answered him You're right.

Little Jack Horner

Little Jack Horner
Sat in the corner
Thumbing his first-grade book.

Look, Jack,
Look at blonde Jane and blue-eyed Dick
And their nice white house
And their nice green lawn
And their nice clean town
And their dog that is brown.

Little Jack Horner,
Dumb in the corner,
Why don't you learn to read?

Little Tom Tucker

Little Tom Tucker
Sang for his school lunch.
What shall we give him?
A budget cut.

Then how shall we give him his vitamins,
And how shall we fill him full?

With starchy rice,
A potato slice,
And ketchup for a fresh vegetable.

A Man of Words

A man of words and not of deeds
Is like a garden full of weeds,
And when the weeds begin to show
It's like a White House full of snow,
And when the snow begins to fall
He does a snow job on us all,
And when we're all out in the cold,
The sunshine of his smile is sold:
The product's sold and oversold.

Fire

Fire! Fire! said Mrs. Dyer:
Where? Where? said Mrs. Dare;
In that part of town, said Mrs. Gown;
Any damage? said Mrs. Gamage;
Only to them, said Mrs. Hem;
So, no worry at all, said Mrs. Hall.

Hey Diddle Diddle

Hey diddle diddle,
Hem haw and fiddle;
How do we integrate?

A jot and a tittle,
Too late and too little,
That's how we integrate.

Hickety, Pickety, My Black Hen

Hickety, pickety, my black hen,
Eggs for ladies and gentlemen,
Breakfast service graciously laid,
Gone with the wind: the sleep-in maid.

Dump It, Dump It

Dump it, dump it, nuclear waste,
Dump it, dump it, better make haste,
The ocean's a hot spot and so is the land:
Don't worry, go bury your head in the sand.

Tom, Tom

Tom, Tom,
Uncle Tom's son;
It's getting harder
To find one.

No more mild and meek
And turn the other cheek,
No more fetch and tote
No more scrape and bow.
Not now.

Not now.

NOT NOW.

The Cow Jumped
Over the Moon

The cow jumped over the moon
On the street in the afternoon.
The junkie laughed to see such sport
With his bag and his needle and spoon.

There Was a Crooked Man

There was a crooked man,
And he did very well.

There Was a Man

There was a man of our town
And he was wondrous wise—

He moved away.

Wisdom

A wise old judge sat in a court,
The case was long, his judgment short.
Why change the way it's always been?
The john goes free, but she's brought in.

I Do Not Like Thee

I do not like thee,
Applicant Fell,
The reason why I cannot tell
Because I'm
An equal opportunity employer.

Twinkie, Twinkie

Twinkie, Twinkie, Mallomar,
Honey-sweet granola bar,
Sugar Smack, Coke, Popsicle sticks:
Need my daily junk food fix.

Numbers

Numbers, run numbers,
What time of day?
One o'clock, two o'clock,
Anytime play.

It's only chicken feed
Poor people pay.
Just pennies and nickels
And two bits they play.

Someday may hit it,
And big they can win . . . !
Until then Mr. Big
Shovels chicken feed in.

Oh Where,
Oh Where Has
My Little Dog Gone?

Oh where, oh where has my little dog gone?
Oh where, oh where can he be?

NO DOGS ALLOWED.

NO BALL PLAYING.

NO LOITERING.

NO PEDDLERS.

NO SOLICITING.

NO BICYCLING.

NO ROLLER SKATING.

NO ENTRANCE AFTER DARK.

NO EXIT.

This is public property.

Pussy Cat,
Pussy Cat,
Where Have You Been?

Pussy cat,
Pussy cat,
Where have you been?
   To the City Hall hearing
   But couldn't get in.
Pussy cat,
Pussy cat,
Why was that?
   It was all about cats
   And their habitats,
   But they only admitted
   Dogs and rats.

Young Flesh to Sell

Young flesh to sell, my flesh to sell,
If I had as much money as I could tell,
I never would cry young flesh to sell,
Young flesh to sell, young and fresh to sell,
I never would cry, young flesh to sell.

Gliding Across

Gliding across
Before the light's green,
Ignoring traffic,
He blots out the scene:

With tapes for
His headset
And skates on
His toes,
Music takes over
Wherever he goes.

Solomon Grundy

Solomon Grundy
Born on Slumday . . .

. . . this is the end
Of Solomon Grundy.

There Was a Little Man

There was a little man and he had a
    little gun
And his bullets were made of lead,
    lead, lead.

He took up his gun and he shot someone
Right through the middle of the head
    head head.

It's so easy to get a gun,
Get a gun, get a gun.
It's so easy to get a gun
And shoot anyone.
Anyone.

The Riddle

What's in there?
　　Gold and money, milk and honey.
Where's my share?
　　The mouse ran away with it.

Where's the mouse?
　　Gone to his house.
Where's his house?
　　Out of this neighborhood
　　Deep in a green, green wood.
Where's the wood?
　　Fire burned it.

Where's the fire?
　　Water quenched it.
Where's the water?
　　The bull cow drank it.

Where's the cow?
　　Behind the hill.
Where's the hill?
　　Covered with snow.
Where did the snow go?
　　Sunshine melted the snow.
Where's the sun?
　　High, high up in the air.
　　Gold and money, milk and honey.
　　There is your share.
　　Up in the air.

Hector Protector

Hector Protector
Did best in the test,
Easily qualified,
Led all the rest.

Hector Protector
Rejected because
The firm wants to show off
Its new hiring clause.

And Hector, though tan
And a proud man of race,
Isn't sufficiently
Black in the face.

Kindness

I love the local pusher
Who's part of my beat,
Whenever I see him
I cross the street.

I do not see a thing,
And I wish him good day;
Who can make ends meet
On just a cop's pay?

Urban Renewal

Urban renewal
Cleans out the slums,
Gets rid of the junkies,
The drunks and the bums;

Clears out the old stuff,
Each crumbling wall,
Clears out the old stuff:
People and all.